To

CW00434458

The Maidenswell Folly

Written and illustrated by Greg Howes

Also by the same author a Gothic/Historical Fiction Novel
"The Man Behind the Glass" (2015)

The Maidenswell Folly

Constance had always been predisposed towards lucid dreams, though one dream in particular caused her a great deal of anxiety. It was not a particularly horrible dream, that is to say, nothing horrific happened within it. It was more the fact that it, or shreds of it, had kept recurring as far back as she could ever remember. Sometimes, the uninvited guest appeared as often as three times in a week, though sometimes it was only a couple of times a month.

Despite the dream being set outside there were walls, rounded walls, made from great blocks of stone and an assortment of large fossils. Constance found them especially intriguing and loved to discover new ones hidden amongst the climbing plants and mortar. So familiar was she with the landscape of the dream, it almost felt like home; although most homes usually had a few human beings in them now and again if not often.

Constance's dream was not bereft of life though, far from it. There were lots of creatures and a plethora of green growth, largely in the form of ivy, moss, and an abundance of tall trees. The fact that it felt so much like home perhaps unsettled her more than anything else. Not all of the sights, sounds and smells remained static though. It was as if she experienced every season with empathy; the withering of the leaves; the tremble of the winds; the bursting of the buds.

She tried hard to come to terms with the dream by telling herself that it was *just* a dream, and *everyone* dreams. Of course they do, though none evidently seemed remotely akin to hers. Constance had spoken to friends and family about her dream over the years, all of whom had had dreams that either frightened or baffled them at one time or another. However, none could empathise with the frequency, or clarity of the dream she had owned since childhood.

Despite her obvious concerns, nobody ever took the matter seriously at all. She had overheard one of her aunts referring to the topic as a form of attention seeking; even her father told her not to yield to it, and told her to stop talking about the dream. "People will think you are an obsessive Constance, worse still, a total bore." With that in mind she vowed never to speak of it to another living soul, with the exception of her boyfriend Dan. Dan was quite fascinated by the dream to begin with, wanting to know every small detail; though recently she felt his interest had begun to wane. It was not that he didn't take her concerns seriously, he did; it was just that his concern had shifted from the contents of the dream to a concern about Constance's mental health. However that was not all; along with that concern, Constance thought she could detect shadows of doubt about their relationship creeping into his expressions too. Alarmingly, she could not point her finger at, or bring to mind one specific instance of his disillusionment in her. Maybe she was obsessing about things; perhaps her father had been right all along? Either that, or she had fallen prey to her insecurities and petty fears. Upon reflection, Constance decided she needed a new challenge; something to distract her from the prosaic nature of her job as a sales clerk, the peculiar dream, and her rightly or wrongly held suspicions about her relationship.

History had long since interested Constance; she marvelled at her grandfather's stories about when he was a guard at the Tower of London. She liked to dig too. She was forever digging holes in the garden as a child, looking for buried treasure and delighting in any old coins she found amongst the worms and mud. With this in mind she had the notion of setting herself an historical quest of her own. Over the years she had spent much time thumbing through historical novels and reading about the history of other people, it was about time she did a little research of her own, and looked into her own family's history for herself. It was, after all, her history too was it not?

Her father's side of the family was quite well known and represented little or no challenge to her, save exploring a few offshoots way back in time. Constance's mother's side was quite a different matter though; her mother's father had come from a largely military family, though evidently, this seemed to have been largely stimulated by the potato famine in Ireland, which saw many a young Irishman throwing his hat into the British Army. She vowed to visit Ireland as soon as she had got to the bottom of the mystery that was her mother's mother's family.

Constance recalled her great aunt Florence saying that she had been told something she was not meant to hear. It was told to her quite surreptitiously by an older member of the family to whom she did allude … that the family once held a

great estate in South West Wales, before moving on to Oxfordshire, whereupon the money had been swiftly lost by bad investments. The investments were supposedly made when the balance of this self same ancestor's mind was disturbed. Constance could not recall Florence saying what caused the upset, if indeed Constance ever asked the question in the first place. Florence had gone on to say that, it was that incident that caused the family to fall from grace and destined them to live a life of *lower middle class mediocrity*, which Florence said she never felt born to at all. When Constance asked her grandmother Sable (Florence's sister), she had dismissed such talk as "Fanciful clap trap", brought on by "too much time on her own and delusions of grandeur". The fact that these rumours were disregarded so quickly had, of course, only sought to inflame Constance's curiosity even more. As a child, Constance knew not how to confirm or deny her aunt's ramblings though now she just may.

Constance's time spent on the Internet, trawling through population census and ordering various birth and marriage certificates had proved very fruitful. As soon as she had discovered that it really was true that one of the branches of her maternal family tree really had owned a noble estate, Constance made plans to visit it immediately. Maidenswell Manor was now a plush hotel and she just had to stay there, even it was only for a couple of nights. She had looked through the spiel on the Internet about the manor; much of the information seemed largely concerned with the healing benefits of strolling through its voluptuous and stately gardens. It had also recently been fitted out with a gym and health spa. They also sold their own bottled water, "Maidenswell Mineral Water", from a source within the estate. The original Well, after which the manor was named, was said to have had magical properties, and helped to perpetuate and retain youth. Constance sighed at the rampant commercialism of it all, and felt that in some inappropriate way, the new owners were lowering the tone of what was now her manor too. There were however a couple of saving graces. At the bottom of the page there was a note mentioning that the manor also contained a reputable library. The library was open to the guests and contained many rare books pertaining to the history of the house and estate. Tours of the house and garden were also available at certain times of the year, upon request.

Due to unforeseen circumstances, Dan could not accompany Constance on her journey which meant she would have to travel to Wales alone. Dan's father had suddenly been taken ill. Although Constance knew this was a perfectly good reason why he could not escort her on the trip, she could not shake off all doubt that he hadn't wanted to accompany her in the first place.

The drive from Oxfordshire to Pembrokeshire in South West Wales had been long and sticky, and after two hundred miles plus of blinding sunshine, Constance was grateful to see that her turn-off was in amongst a leafy grove of trees. The manor was situated near the hamlet of Pwll-yr-Gwarach. A strange name she thought, roughly translating as The Old Crone's/Witch's Pool. Constance had tried to pronounce it endlessly since first seeing it on the map. The peculiar thing was though, now that she was within touching distance of the hamlet, she said the words out loud, and they came out perfectly, without the slightest effort or hesitation.

The lush and dappled canopy that Constance had initially found refreshing, now seemed endless and somewhat claustrophobic. She was sure the sign said the hamlet was but three miles ahead; how could it be? It felt more like six and there was still no sign of any hamlet or manor at all: not one house, shed, or even any traffic. *Perhaps I failed to spot a turn? There was evidence of one a while back, though that looked much more like an old and redundant farm track, not a way to a hotel such as Maidenswell Manor. Maybe I missed it*, she thought to herself, whilst looking to see if she had any new text messages on her phone. She was determined to turn around when the road next widened, which surely it must do soon. *Either the atmosphere around the trees has changed, or I have.* The further Constance drove, the faster she went: nervous and urgent. Her once benign troop of trees now felt palpably and inexplicably hostile towards her: tightening around her like a giant arboreal fist.

Without rhyme or reason a group of crows suddenly swooped down from their lofty perch, directly in front of the car, scarcely missing Constance's windscreen. Her foot slammed down upon the brakes, causing the car to skid across the road violently. She narrowly avoided sliding onto the verge and waited in silence for another vehicle to run into her from behind, momentarily forgetting that she has not seen one in front of her or behind her for miles.

Constance dared to look behind; there was no one there. *This is deepest Wales*, she told herself, *not the M25 motorway.* She got out of the car and looked around her. Luckily three of the car's wheels were still on the road and not submerged into the boggy verge. *This is where I will turn around. It may take a few attempts, though I can do it if I'm careful. Thank god Dan isn't here to see me try though*, she groaned inwardly.

Constance was about to get into the car again when she saw something pale and solid ahead of her. It was neither tree nor tarmac, a farm perhaps? *This has to be worth a look,* she thought.

The thing ahead of her turned out not to be a farm; it was the first of a pair of Georgian gate-houses, in front of which was a sign pointing to the hamlet of Pwll-yr-Gwarach. As she drove closer she was relieved to see a large sign saying Maidenswell Manor Hotel. The sign was partially obscured by the exuberant spring growth of a clump of wild rhubarb, or *Gunnera*, as her father told her they should really be called. The two columns supporting the vast iron gates were topped with mighty iron dragons looking towards the avenue ahead.

"At last!" Constance said out loud. She was now where she should be. She drove slowly up the long drive, windows open, surveying the multihued rhododendrons and azaleas that were interspersed among a fine selection of noble pines, oaks, limes, birch and ash. She was certain she saw a bullfinch out of the corner of her eye, though it was difficult to swear to as there were so many birds darting here and there.

All her anxiety had fled. *Here I can find peace amongst the birdsong and wonder of the place. The air is heavy and still, and every now and again I can just about detect the heady fragrance of an orange blossom tree. I can also smell the*

13

rather sickly scent of ivy, which is strange because the scent of ivy is rarely pungent unless it is in flower, or you happen to be very close to its source. How strange it is that I can almost taste it now, despite the fact that it is far too early for it to be in flower, and the only the sign of the climber is some way off in the distance, meandering its way up a venerable oak. Unnervingly, it is one of the most familiar odours of my dream, though I refuse to dwell on the matter now. There is far too much intrigue ahead to waste time dwelling on such a detail as that.

After parking, Constance wrote Dan a text message:
"Hi Dan, I've arrived safely. Very hot here. Send my love to your Dad and wish him a speedy recovery on my behalf. Missing you, love you lots, Constance xx"

There is still no signal here, though surely the text will send itself later when the signal returns, will it not? she surmised, hopefully.

She was greeted at the hotel by a receptionist with high auburn hair and huge pearl earrings.
"Oh yes, you are the lady whose family once owned the house?"
"Yes I believe so; I have only just found this out. I've driven up from Oxfordshire today. It's a beautiful house."
"Yes it is, so easy to get lost here though, so many rooms," said the lady with the pearly earrings and smile to match.

"You are in room twenty-five, on the fourth floor; it is situated in one of the older parts of the manor, lovely view of the garden and the woods beyond."

"Thank you very much, I look forward to seeing how much it has changed," Constance replied eagerly with a hint of bedevilment.

"Ha ha yes, you are very welcome Miss Reid. I hope you enjoy your stay. The stairs are over there, though there is a lift through those doors." The pearly lady pointed with a pearl ringed finger to a room yonder.

"Before I go, could you please tell me where I would find the library? I'd love to find out more about my family and this estate."

"Of course, if you head towards the lift and get off at the second floor, you will see the signs. It shuts at five though, so you have only about an hour and half left if you wish to borrow anything. We do have this though if you miss it." The receptionist gave her a rather thin brochure with a photo of the sauna on the front.

"There is not a great deal of history in it, but it should keep you going until the library opens up again in the morning. Peter, who is in charge, usually gets here about nine thirty; there's nothing that man does not know about the estate. Not that you would think it to look at him, needs a new tailor too I reckon," joked the receptionist, somewhat unkindly thought Constance. "If I were you though I would check out the garden first, leave the studying until the morning. Rain's coming in tonight so they say. It will be ruthless with the roses I dare say. Do you like roses?"

"Umm, yes. I do, especially in somebody else's garden, can't abide the thorns. I love the darker ones myself, not so keen on the floribundas. A job to beat a hybrid tea though eh?"

16

The receptionist simply smiled vacantly. Constance deduced that the receptionist had reached the end of her knowledge of the species *Rosa*, so she grabbed her bag and said,
"Thank you for that, I will see you again shortly I am sure."
"Yes dear, hope you have a lovely night."

Constance opted to walk up the stairs; her bag was not particularly heavy, besides she would hate to miss out on any of the manor's interior on her ascent. In fact, she wanted to imbibe every last drop every of her new surroundings. She studied the portraits keenly on her way up the stairs, vainly looking out for similarities in face or form. She chided herself for absurdly trying to find familiarity within the unfamiliar. *I've never been to the old manor before, so why on earth am I trying to find commonplace? Despite that, there is yet a tenacious sense of home here. At first I thought I was sharing the same ludicrous sense of delusions of grandeur that had engulfed my great aunt Florence. Conversely it's not that at all, quite the opposite. Instead of liberation, there is a cloying sense of duty; instead of opulence, there is confinement. Nothing I've seen has brought back any specific recollections, save for a brief flash of familiarity whilst driving past the gatehouses, something I accredit to having seen on the website.*

Room twenty-five was everything she hoped it was would be: wonderfully light, airy and unspoilt. Two huge sash windows lent themselves to a stunning view across the manicured lawn, the pleasure garden and the dense woodland beyond. The room smelt vaguely of lavender, which for no apparent reason she had thought it may. Apart from the bed, most of the furniture within the bedchamber was antique. She felt oddly enthralled by one of the high back chairs. It was made from some kind of a dark wood, with crimson velvet upholstery encased in light gold braid. She surely had seen that chair before; that at least was familiar to her. As Constance started to unpack she was distracted by the sound of a family making merry outside of her window. She made her way over to the window and peered out. There were some people out on the lawn sat on a large Persian rug. She smiled when she saw them. *Oh it's only Papa and Mamma, little Georgie, oh, and Theodora too. I can't see that little fidget staying there for long,* she laughed. Upon seeing her, Georgie waved and shouted something that was lost to the wind.

It was not until she turned away from the window that the utter insanity of the moment struck home. By the time she rushed back to the window there was nobody to be seen. *There's no way on earth that anyone could have left the lawn so quickly,* she thought. How had she known their names? She scanned the horizon looking for clues of their whereabouts. There were none. She relinquished her watch and lay upon the bed. *Surely there's no sense in any of this?* she thought. *I definitely saw a family there; I can even recall the style of the hamper and the colour of the dress on the woman she called... Mamma? But the grand lady resembles my mother not one iota.*

Dan had been surprised by his father's heart attack. He always thought him so fit, totally bomb proof if he was honest. It had come totally out of the blue and he had spent the last two days driving back and forth to the hospital. Now that his father was on the mend, Dan hoped to drive up to

Wales tomorrow and give Constance a nice surprise. He had felt quite deflated that he could not join her on her quest, but his father's health came first. Dan had witnessed such disappointment in Constance's eyes when she realised that he would not be able make the trip with her. Of course, she had tried valiantly to hide it. Although Constance had never spoken to him of doing anything other than "the right thing" by his father, or for him not to be there with his dad at the hospital, he still sensed an uncomfortable feeling of resentment there, left unsaid. It was no secret that his father did not like Constance very much. "Too flaky by half," he said. Dan knew it would not have been a good idea asking her to come with him, which in fairness to her she may well have done if he had insisted, but she had not really met his father much and when she had, his dad had been less than generous with his welcome. Beside that, she had been so anxious of late, this break was just what she needed. Constance had been a different girl since her recent discovery; it was as if all her troubles had evaporated instantly. *And after all, who am I to stop her?* he mused with a smile.

Dan was elated that his father had recovered faster than expected and that the consultant thought he could be out of hospital sometime tomorrow. His sister said she would pick their father up later on tomorrow if progress was still being made. As soon as Dan got the good news he began making plans to follow Constance to Wales tomorrow. He had sworn the Hotel's receptionist to secrecy in the matter and could not help but picture Constance's face when he arrived.

Dan was pleased to have been able to send off an email with some of the information from the book Constance had ordered about the manor. She had been so disappointed when the book had not arrived prior to her departure. *Hopefully*, he thought, *she will read the email before she starts exploring the house and grounds later. I'm surprised that I've only received one text message from Constance since her arrival at the manor. Though upon reflection, I doubt her mobile phone's signal is reliable at the hotel, given that it's so far off the beaten track.*

The incident with the family outside her window left Constance agitated and confused. She tried to remember the family's forenames that she found on the eighteen forty-one census returns. All of the family except for the eldest daughter (who had probably married) had moved to Oxfordshire by the time of the nineteen hundred and fifty-one census returns. Her ancestor was a George, she was sure of it, though could not be sure of the other two children. She must go downstairs and see if she could find the family in the gardens. Constance took the lift downstairs and set about exploring the beauteous grounds. *How I wish Dan was here,* she thought. *I am sure he would have made sense of all this. Maybe I just made up those names when I saw that family? After all, I did not call out their names did I? The small boy waved up as if he knew me, did he not? Though, how do I know it was me he was looking at? It may have been someone else he waved at, in a different window?* Doubts such as these swarmed around Constance's mind like discontented bees.

Initially, Constance walked quickly along a myriad of twisting pathways, peering inquisitively through leafy boughs and flower drenched shoots; so desperate was she for a glimpse of the vanishing family. After a very short while, she found her agitation beginning to wane, if not her curiosity. The garden was absorbing her pore by pore, step by step. It was as though she was entering upon a dance. At first her steps were unsure, perplexed as to what form it may take and where they may lead. Little by little her resistance was undone and her hesitance brushed aside by a scented floral comb.

The repressive nature of the house had been replaced by an overwhelming feeling of liberation. The song of the grounds ushered her into the very private world of the walled garden. *This,* she felt, was her inner sanctum of deliverance, a symphony to call her own. The lime washed walls of still earth were her shield, the pond, her personal mirror, framed with lilies and light. Azure damselflies were her ladies in waiting, embroiled as they were in the minuet of the moment. In the centre of the pond stood a lazy fountain, gently pouring forth the divine gift of the sky. Ripples arose and span languidly outward before becoming lost in their own soporific sojourns.

There is not another soul to be seen here and that is how it should be, she mused. *I hate it when others invade my own special place - except for the gardener Nathaniel; he is always such an integral part of the walled garden. He is part of its weave. He never speaks unless spoken to, not I feel out of deference. No, it is just that he seems so infatuated with his work, and to leave it would almost be sinful to him. He has the devotion of a priest, or an artist even, perhaps more so; though unlike an artist, who perhaps envisages hours, days, weeks ahead of them, this man sees years into the future. He*

has worked here for decades as had his father and grandfather before him. Of course his wiles were born out of the past but they were made manifest in the present. Nathaniel never ever neglects the present, how could he? I'm sure it sings to him through his eyes as it does to me now. Every single seed sown or seedling planted is never just that, it is foreseen to be a towering oak, a noble bay or a majestic climbing red rose, written on the wall years before it inspires a lover's pluck.

"What an odd thought," Constance exclaimed. Odder still that it probably was not her own and yet it bothered her not. Perhaps this was the Well in which the rivers of the past and present ran into. *What an exciting notion, I wonder what Dan would think of that.*

The only doorway besides that of the entrance to the walled garden led to the fernery. Constance needed not to have read the rustic sign telling her so. If she found liberation amongst the grounds, sanctuary in the walled garden, repression in the manor, the fernery was a place for dreams, a place for secrets. It truly was the "other world", the place where she used to sit beholden in the twilight of its mottled glass. A space of almost liquid definition, a place where there was no exact good or truly bad, just green: a fairy green, a tropical jungle green, a green that was only true to its hue, and itself. Here dwelt the mysterious and silent creeping mosses and ferns, whose tongues seemed to spring out of nowhere, yet yielded a language known upon earth. Within this sentient emerald lay a small ornamental waterfall, though Constance knew it to be really a harp. A harp deftly played by a conjurer, one who could place you upon a string and take you across the oceans

of your mind with one swift movement of a skilful finger; through fearsome and beautiful forests, desolate, hoary crested peaks of virtue and deep down again; under the seas of guilt to the hidden places, the anemone bejewelled caves of the maids of Mer and beyond. Fantastical places every one, given freely by the fernery and never by your own design. She closed her eyes and gave herself to the room in all its opiate glory.

Constance awoke with a jolt. How long she had been asleep she could not tell. In her fervour to find the strange and elusive family she had left her mobile phone behind in her bedroom. Not that it really mattered, she thought, there was hardly any signal here for messaging, and as far as food was concerned she could eat later. If the hotel had stopped serving dinner she could have a bar snack later, not that she was in the least bit hungry for the time being. The sleep had left her feeling somewhat bewildered. She thought it quite astonishing that she had been quite so compliant to the call of the gardens, in spite of their unarguable charm. The family may have eluded her for the present, but had she, in the meantime, found herself? It was all quite difficult to make sense of. Constance certainly felt she had been here before. Maybe she had come here as a child, that would explain the vision of the old gardener and the childlike wonder that she had experienced earlier. If that was the case though why had her mother not told her? Surely it would have rung a bell with her; after all she knew I was coming here. *How I wish she possessed as much interest in our family's history as I have,* Constance mused, ruefully. *If it was not the case that I have been here before, maybe I visited here in a past life? Or perhaps I really was connecting with some past ancestral*

memory, one that had only been resurrected by my presence at the manor? So many questions, and as yet so few answers.

The sun had slipped a little in the sky, though it was still strong enough to sear Constance's eyes when she stepped warily out of the verdant clutches of magical fernery. The gentle rhythm of the walled garden still hummed softly in her ear; and the bumble bees darted in and out of the plentiful flowers playfully, as though, she thought, they were occupied in their own private game of hide and seek. The garden seemed at peace with itself and she tried very hard to rejoin with its song, though for some reason it eluded her. Initially, she considered there to be something amiss from the melody, but upon contemplation it was not that, the sound was still as splendid and complete a tune as it ever was. The truth was that there appeared to be another song calling out to her from out beyond the sanctuary of the walled garden. It sounded as though it was woman's voice though she could not be totally sure of the matter. Although it sounded very much akin to a lament, she was both enchanted by its sound and intrigued as to its provenance. The sound possessed an inherent and unique loneliness all of its own. Despite its disconsolate disposition, its resonance conjured up an uncountable number of images within the eye of her mind. An island far out at sea, with a halo of gulls, spare of life save for spiny wind swept growths, withered in vigour and bedraggled in aspect. Tough grasses were interspersed with broken stones; were they ruined altars or giant's teeth, knocked out by a sea bound Titan long ago? She saw visions of the breeze running its fingers timorously through the bulrushes at the autumn of the day. Rivulets of molten bronze sweeping westward towards

27

an isolated estuary, exalted by the blood and embers of the dying sun.

Instead of being repelled by such forlorn images Constance felt uncannily drawn towards their source. Once out of the sanctity of the walled garden she felt compelled to make a decision: whether to find the provenance of this mesmeric call, or return to the manor. *I really ought to ring Dan and grab some supper. What the devil would he make of this strange place and the even stranger me for that matter*, she mused jovially. She looked skyward as if seeking guidance from up on high. There were dark plumes of clouds to the west, though their descent looked far from imminent. *It would not take long to seek out the place of this curious beckoning. I may not have another chance*, she mused. Constance was aware of the absurdity of it, but she was here now, besides, it may rain for the rest of the weekend and the frustration of not having gone would drive her insane.

She sailed her way through islands of bamboos and feathered palms, past the sunken icehouse to the borderlands, where the wild reaches of the forest met the decorative hand of man. While crossing the invisible bridge between the two worlds a strange thought entered her mind. Whether it was the past murmuring deep and uncorked in the cellars of her mind, or something that she had been warned of in an earlier visit (should such a visit ever have taken place?) she was not sure. It was not only a thought, it was an image too, that of the elderly gardener, the one with the far sight she had mused upon earlier. She felt like he was with her now, upon the precipice.

"If you have a mind to go further, think again missy, it is not your place to be out there…Too easy to get lost you see. It is much wetter than you think it is. Go back to the garden or manor if you wish, you are safe there." It was, just as though for a second, he was right there in front of her - his moist brow, walnut furled and weather worn. He wore such a look upon his face, one that Constance had seen before, stern and masterful, yet sentience radiated from it, as a lilac would its scent. It was a frightful look. No wonder it was still playing upon her fancy after all these years, she yielded. As he spoke, or as she recalled his words anyway, the delicate melody that had so seduced her steps momentarily ceased. It was as though it had been banished by this gnarled and woody old man. There followed such a cavernous silence that she felt as if the entire whole world had been swallowed up by its vast and incalculable emptiness.

A solitary magpie broke the silence and flew out from within the clutches of a stoic old cedar tree. The bird flew deep into the beckoning and primitive wood beyond the garden's breadth. Its stuttering flight took it towards the knots of charcoal and cinder coloured clouds that had been gathering stealthily to the west. Just as the old rustic's words of warning had broken the spell of the lilting lament, the flight of the magpie had, in some unknowable way, re-ignited the rapture within Constance's soul. Her determination reinforced, inexplicably so, by the magpie's jaunt. The vision of the old gardener and his words seemed nothing more than a distant memory now.

It was not that she was oblivious to the threat of rain on the horizon, she was not. Its liquid intentions gave her wings to

each and every footfall. Not even the increasingly torn and tangled path could deter her voracious passage. The call that was driving her fleetness of foot was becoming forever louder, and even more forlorn. Perversely, Constance questioned as to whether the reverberations were audible to any other person or creature other than herself? Or was she the solitary catalyst that gave texture and form to something that would be otherwise intangible, beyond comprehension to another?

Oddly, the further she ran away from the garden the more familiar everything became. This was the sensory environment that she had always known since birth, imbued within the dream. She skipped passed foxgloves, willow herbs and flower-spent bluebells. The blooms had now become that of the margins, those of the wood. She also noticed remnants from long ago, when the garden was broader and less concentrated around the manor house. Abandoned and crumbling statuettes peered out through algae stained eyes, virtually hidden by the ever-encroaching wilderness. Box trees, once the subject for skilled and wondrous topiary, now sprouted out chaotically, misshapen relics, long since neglected by the sun and blade alike. A few scouting raindrops dashed against her cheek and for the first time today she actually felt somewhat cold. Her eyes took on the expression of the hunter and the hunted, wide, sharp and alert. She sensed the path contracting with every footfall; it seemed as though the branches were lashing out, confused as to whether to bind her or chastise her for her flight.

A couple of rummaging squirrels fled her path, surprised at the sudden intrusion. *This is not a well frequented way*, she reluctantly mused. An involuntary shudder ran through her veins causing her to lose her stride. Whether it was a symptom of the chill wind, or her body reacting to some unperceived threat or fear that she was neglecting, Constance could not tell. She felt near to her goal now, unstoppable. The sky had changed so much since she set off. Relentless storm clouds had hastened the onset of twilight. The once coloured birds that flew about her were now all totally black, silhouetted against the ever darkening cinders of the day. Raindrops had smudged Constance's vision of truth so much that the beautiful shapes of the birds above were now no more than grotesques of liquid jet.

Up ahead there was a fork in the path. The more open and shallower of the two tracks veered off steadily to the right, whilst the other, much deeper and densely clothed with briars and bramble, led to the left, up towards a small mound. Upon that mound, barely visible from the path, lay an old ruin. There was no choice to be made. Constance's inexplicable urgency to embrace the source of this sorrowful yet mesmeric call was beyond her reasoning; yet in some unfathomable way she almost became one with it. She was suddenly astonished at having caught herself singing the lament too. It was not something she had been aware of and wondered just how long she had been doing such a thing. She tore her way through the undergrowth feverously, like a fox evading bloodthirsty hounds. Her bare arms were being scratched remorselessly by dense thickets of dog rose and holly.

Constance's nostrils became full of the scent of elderflower, which was the "Tree of Witches", or so she had read. Her stout boots were holding out well despite the wetness all

around. The spiteful nettles and thorns were out in force, and she had lost count of how many times she had either been cut or stung. Not that she cared; she was now oblivious to pain. The further up the mound she scaled the wetter the earth beneath her became. It oozed out of the ground malevolently. There was a cracking of twigs and one of her feet slipped upon the bank. She viewed the ruinous mass before her in awe. This was the place of her dreams. "At last…I have found you!" Constance yelled out; wracked with emotion, tears cascading down her face. She held her fists up high in the air; her leaf-stained hands torn and muddy. Feelings of relief, horror, elation and utter disbelief engulfed her. Constance ran her soiled fingers down her face, before continuing her urgent quest to the top of the marshy mount.

The building in front of her was that of a Folly: something she knew to have been a purpose built ruin, fashionable in the eighteenth century. She should have known that was what it was all along, but it was only now that the word *folly* came to her. Despite the Folly being deliberately erected as a ruin there was no pretence needed now; almost half of its decaying stonework was covered in ivy, woody stems clothed in soft shields of green. Constance's tear-stained cheeks glistened as long streaks of rain splashed upon her face. Dotted amongst the great stone blocks were huge fossils, ammonites and trilobites and many others she had either forgotten or had never learnt. She walked inside the door-less entrance. *It's so frighteningly muddy here*, she thought. She instinctively looked aloft; there she espied a magpie, looking down upon her in earnest from its lofty perch. Although the magpie was the only bird she saw it was not however the only bird she witnessed. Unseen, she heard the awful laughing noise

emanating from a flock or "murder" of crows close by. Their malignant cries were accompanied only by the hissing of the tall trees that encircled the ruin. She took a laborious step forward, taking her deeper into the black heart of the Folly. The forest floor was cloying and grew heavy beneath her feet. It was saturated. She felt the hungry earth beneath sucking her downwards. A solitary lamb cried out far off in the distance…

Dan's e-mail (unsent during the day) arrived to Constance's smart phone at 10.00 Friday night:

"I sent this message to you earlier babe, and for some reason it did not send, so here it is again. I have tried texting you in the meantime but I cannot seem to get through to you. I imagine you are far too busy checking out your new stately home, lol."

"Hi Constance ☺
Just in case you have not read up on the origins of the house yet. Maidenswell Manor as you may already know was named after a notable Well now lost. Although lost the Well was thought to lie between the hamlet of Pwll-yr-Gwarach (try saying that after a bottle or two of wine) and the present day manor. So that is your task for the day, to locate the Well, lol. A Roman source said the Well (and its waters) were both feared and venerated by the local Celts. Apparently, the present day manor house was situated on the site of an old Monastery, the monks of which became unsettled due to the local folk's continuing belief that the Well was of magical

*origin. They believed that the Well still contained a powerful
and fearful deity, so the monks wishing to dispel such heathen
beliefs for good decided have the Well consecrated. Not only
did they consecrate the Well the monks dedicated it to some
saint or another, the name escapes me at the moment.
Anyway, the crux of the matter was that things did not go as
the monks planned. According to one story the water swiftly
turned poisonous and killed the Abbot the very next day. Over
the next hundred or so years there were many unexplained
disappearances and mishaps attributed to the "angry" Well,
that led to both monk and villager alike setting about
breaking the Well's stone surround. The village elders laid
out a set of rules saying that, not only was it strictly forbidden
to place votive offerings around the land where the Well once
lay, it was also strictly forbidden to attempt to draw water
from, or clear the area around the Well for any purpose
whatsoever; any person who broke these rules would incur a
very severe punishment. According to one scribe it was hoped
that, in the fullness of time, by the grace of god, that the
poisonous Well would be forgotten and returned to the
wilderness, along with any woeful tales accredited to it.
Judging by this it is clearly not the case eh babe?*

*Oh I nearly forgot to say, and this is right up your street, on
the outskirts of the estate there is a Folly, dating back to the
mid seventeen fifties, built by one of your newly found landed
ancestors. My, how posh are you? Apparently, one Gerald
Morgan's daughter absconded into the woods after a family
argument and was never seen again. It was said to have been
a frightful and ungodly night. There had been much rain and
the earth was soaked to dreadful proportions. Search parties
were sent out in all directions at dawn, and the whole estate*

joined in with the search. It was not long before the estate's gardener found a set of recently made footprints upon one of the trails that led through the estate. The hunt for the girl led them to a wild area within the woods, whereupon they followed the footsteps towards the top of a small marshy rise in the landscape. Her footprints were alleged to have been uncannily deep due to the wetness of the ground. The woody marsh led to what was considered to be nothing more than a diminutive pond, though that pond had swollen dreadfully by the deluge of water.

Strangely, the footsteps headed directly into the pond. Mysteriously, no body was ever found and the wayward daughter was never seen again. Some, of course, believed that she met her lover here, but there was no evidence to suggest that at all. Reluctantly, as the months went by she was presumed drowned. Anyway, the heart-broken Gerald decided to leave a monument to his beloved daughter, so he built a Folly at the very top of the mound amongst the marshy woods. Can you imagine the work? His daughter (like you) had always been captivated by fossils, and he had amassed a vast collection over the years. The doting father had his entire collection built into the structure of the folly, so if her spirit still resided there she would have something close by for her to cherish for all time. Such a sad story to finish on but never fear…I hope to see you tomorrow darling, yes tomorrow. Dad is so much better so I am free to come down. I was going to keep it as a surprise for you, as I know how much you love surprises; but oh well; I just could not wait to tell you the good news ☺

Lots of love Dan XXX"

About the Author

Greg Howes is an author, genealogist and poet based in Carmarthenshire, South West Wales, UK. Greg has lived in Carmarthenshire for the last twenty-five years, though he originates from Thame in Oxfordshire, England, UK.

He is the author of the Gothic/Historical fiction novel "The Man Behind the Glass". Greg's work as a historical researcher has seen him present (and research for) family history programmes on television for both the BBC and ITV channels. He has taught family history (and horticulture, in his younger days) and featured on national and local radio stations, answering questions and giving advice on family history and the historical landscape.

He has written many articles for various magazines on subjects as diverse as local history, dating and archiving old photographs, and the history of woodland and ancient trees in the landscape. Greg is also a published poet and a designer of largely black and white prints for book covers, posters and CDs

www.themanbehindtheglass.co.uk

www.welshfamilyhistory.co.uk/index.php

www.facebook.com/Greg-J-Howes-373322379511245/